W9-ARZ-092

SUPER ANGRY
BIRDS

Become our fan on Facebook facebook.com/idwpublishing
Follow us on Twitter @idwpublishing
Subscribe to us on YouTube youtube.com/idwpublishing
See what's new on Tumblr tumblr.idwpublishing.com
Check us out on Instagram instagram.com/idwpublishing

COVER ART BY
MARCELO FERREIRA

COVER COLORS BY
DIEGO RODRIGUEZ

COLLECTION EDITS BY
JUSTIN EISINGER
AND ALONZO SIMON

PUBLISHER
TED ADAMS

COLLECTION DESIGN BY
CHRIS MOWRY

Thanks to Jukka Heiskanen, Juha Mäkinen, and the Rovio team for their hard work and invaluable assistance.

Mikael Hed, Executive Producer
Laura Nevanlinna, Publishing Director
Mikko Pöllä, Creative Director
Jukka Heiskanen, Editor-in-Chief, Comics
Juha Mäkinen, Editor, Comics
Antti Meriluoto, Senior Graphic Designer
Henrik Sarimo, Graphic Designer
Nathan Cosby, Freelance Editor

978-1-63140-549-5   19 18 17 16   1 2 3 4

SUPER ANGRY BIRDS. MARCH 2016. FIRST PRINTING.

Originally published as SUPER ANGRY BIRDS issues #1–4.

Ted Adams, CEO & Publisher
Greg Goldstein, President & COO
Robbie Robbins, EVP/Sr. Graphic Artist
Chris Ryall, Chief Creative Officer/Editor-in-Chief
Matthew Ruzicka, CPA, Chief Financial Officer
Dirk Wood, VP of Marketing
Lorelei Bunjes, VP of Digital Services
Jeff Webber, VP of Licensing, Digital and Subsidiary Rights
Jerry Bennington, VP of New Product Development

For international rights, please contact licensing@idwpublishing.com

Written by:
Jeff Parker (Issues #1 & 3)
and Paul Tobin (Issue #2 & 4)

Art by:
Ron Randall

Colors by:
Jeremy Colwell

Letters by:
Pisara Oy

Edited for Rovio by:
Jukka Heiskanen, Juha Mäkinen
& Nathan Cosby

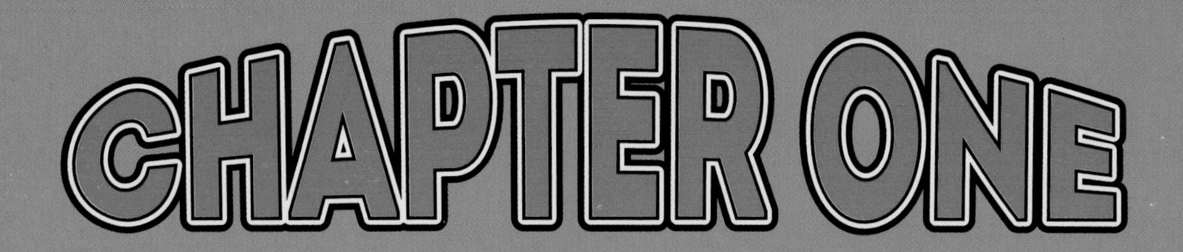

CHAPTER ONE

ARTWORK BY RON RANDALL
COLORS BY ANTTI MERILUOTO

HOT SANDWICHES! PIZZA! PICK UP LUNCH HERE!
FOUR GRILLED CHEESES, PLEASE!
THESE ARE DELICIOUS! I'VE BEEN WAITING FOR YOU TO SET UP ON OUR BLOCK!
NOTHING FOR ME, I'VE GOT TO GET BACK TO THE GREENHOUSE.
PIZZA!
H-HEY! SIR, YOU NEED TO PAY FOR THAT FIRST!
GAAH!
IT HAD TRUFFLE HERBS IN IT! I'M ALLERGIC TO THEM!
HAH! SERVES THAT THUG RIGHT FOR STEALING FOOD.
OH NO!
YOU BETTER MOVE THE CART SOMEWHERE ELSE, LADY.
THAT WAS ONE OF KING PIG'S GANG!
I WAS JUST TRYING TO DO BUSINESS...
VVRROOOM!
CLEAR OUT!

WHBAASSH!
YOW!
YOU'RE SHUT DOWN! HAR HARRR!
MY KITCHEN!
BE RIGHT BACK!
THEY COULD HAVE KILLED ME!
DON'T EVEN THINK OF SETTING UP SHOP IN THIS PART OF TOWN AGAIN.
ESPECIALLY SELLING THAT SLOP!
NOW CLEAN DIS MESS UP OR WE'LL HAVE THE COPS SLAP A FINE ON...
...WHY ARE YOU GOING DOWN?
I'M NOT, YOU'RE GOING UP!

THE FOLKS IN THIS TOWN HAVE HAD ENOUGH OF BEING BULLIED-
-AND THAT'S OUR FAVORITE FOOD CART!
IT'S THE ANGRY BIRDS! THEY'RE REAL!
SUPER ANGRY BIRDS
WE SURE ARE, KID!
THE EAGLE'S EYE

FSSSSSSH!
TOO BAD FOR YOU MY BUDDY BOMB HAS A SHORT FUSE.
YEP.

EYOWW!
I'M BOILIN'!
OWOWOWOWOWOW-

OKAY, THUNDER.
LIKE THEY SAID, GET RID OF THIS MESS.

THAT WAS KING PIG'S FAVORITE CAR!
CRASH!

AND THIS--
--IS OUR FAVORITE--
--LUNCH CART!
OH WOW! IT'S LIKE NEW!
A LITTLE BETTER ACTUALLY, I FIXED ONE OF THE BURNERS ON YOUR STOVE.

AREN'T THEY GREAT?
I'D SAY THEY'RE **SENSATIONAL.**

FOOMF
LIKE **FRONT PAGE** GOOD.

GRRRR...
THE EAGLE'S EYE
BIRD VIGILANTES DEAL WITH THUGS
I CAN'T NEVER FINISH THAT CROSS-WORD PUZZLE!
AND WHO ARE THESE COSTUMED BIRDS BUTTIN' INTO MY BUSINESS?!
WE AIN'T BEEN ABLE TO FIND OUT, KING!
BUT THERE'S THE PUBLISHER OF THE EAGLE'S EYE...
OLD MIGHTY.
HE KNOWS EVERYTHING GOING DOWN IN NEW YOLK, DON'T HE?
HMM. YEAH.
SNOUTS, GO ASK OLD MIGHTY WHEN HIS PAPER IS GOING TO EXPOSE THESE TROUBLEMAKERS.
EEP!

EH... MR. MIGHTY, MY BOSS WAS WONDERIN'...
IT DOESN'T CONCERN ME OR THE CITY PAPER. WE DON'T ANSWER TO ANYONE.
EVEN *THE CRIME BOSS OF NEW YOLK.*
THE EAGLE SAID-
YOU TELL HIM THAT DISTRIBUTION IS HARD TO MAINTAIN AND COULD...DRY UP.
THE BOSS-
MY HEARING MUST BE BAD BECAUSE THAT ***SOUNDED*** LIKE A THREAT!
TELL HIM THAT'S BECAUSE IT ***IS!***
YOU DON'T RUN ***EVERYTHING*** IN THIS CITY YET!
BUT THE CHEF HERE IS MY UNCLE!
AND IF YOU WANT SARDINE PASTA TO STAY ON THE MENU, I WANT TO READ AN EXPOSÉ ON THESE ANGRY BIRDS!
FINE, IT'LL HAPPEN!
AND STOP MAKIN' THE PUZZLES SO HARD!

GET BACK OUT THERE, FIND OUT EVERYTHING YOU CAN ON THE ANGRY GANG.
WE'RE GOING TO RUN A FEATURE ON THEM.
WHAT-REALLY?
BUT THEY'RE BUSTIN' UP KING PIG'S RACKETS, THE ONES THE COPS NEVER TOUCH.
FASCINATING.
I DUNNO, IT SEEMS LIKE WE'VE FINALLY GOT A WAY TO FIGHT CORRUPTION...
CORRUPTION IS THE NEW DEMOCRACY, RAY.
THESE ANGRIES ARE JUST OUT FOR THEMSELVES LIKE EVERYBODY ELSE.
DRIVE.
GUESS I'LL START WITH THE ONES WHO SEE EVERYTHING IN THIS 'BURG.

HOW'S IT GOING, BOYS!
GREAT, CHUCK. DIDJA GET TODAY'S PAPER?
YEAH, ALREADY HAVE IT ON THE WALL.
YOU HEAR OF ANY TROUBLE WE NEED TO KNOW ABOUT?
BOY, HAVE WE, CHECK IT OUT...
THE EAGLE
A LOT OF THE FOOTWORK IS DONE BY THE RIGHT GUY FOR THE JOB, NAMED CHUCK.
NOT EASY TO KEEP UP WITH.
EVEN HARDER WHEN HE CHANGES INTO HIS ALTER EGO...
CHASER!

BUT I PAID THE METER!
I'M IN A HUR-- EE!
IT'S HARD TO REMEMBER, BUT NEW YOLK WAS ONCE A NICE CITY TO LIVE IN.
TAXI
UNTIL THE PIGS WORKED THEIR WAY INTO EVERY POSITION OF POWER.
AND THEN A FEW MONTHS AGO, WE STARTED HEARING REPORTS OF NEW BIRDS IN TOWN.
EVERYBODY CLEAR THE STREET! THE SKY IS FALLING!
BIRDS WHO WEREN'T CONTENT TO LET THE CITY JUST KEEP COMING DOWN.
CRUNCH!
OMIGOSH!
I GOT YA!

THAT'S RED. HE'S PRETTY IMPORTANT, BUT I'LL GET BACK TO HIM LATER.
CHASER, GET BOMB UP THERE!
GET IN POSITION, BOMB!
BUT I FINALLY GOT TO MY SANDWICH!
SING IT, STELLA!
THE NEXT GUY IS PRETTY VOLATILE. BUT HE'S NOT ALWAYS A HOTHEAD, AS I FOUND OUT WHEN I FOUND THEM IN PLAIN CLOTHES LATER THAT NIGHT.
HE AND CHASER WORK TOGETHER WELL, I'D SAY.
GOING UP!
HOLDING MY FUSE...
...AS LONG AS I CAN....

I DON'T KNOW THE WHOLE STORY, BUT HE MOVED INTO TOWN AND DIDN'T LIKE WHAT HE SAW.
OH GOSH!
SO HE BROUGHT IN HIS POWERFUL FRIENDS AND STARTED MAKING IT CLEAR TO THE PIGS...
KWHAMM!
THE BIRDS ARE BACK IN TOWN... AND THEY'RE ANGRY!
GHEE!
HOORRAAYY!
YAYYY BIRDS!
WHAT'S THEIR AGENDA, I WONDER.
THEY LOOK KINDA MEAN!
START GETTING SERIOUS ABOUT SAFETY CODES!
IT AIN'T OUR FAULT, THAT BUILDING PASSED PIGSPECTION-
OW!
THESE BIRDS LIKE BEING CONSIDERED HEROES, THAT'S CLEAR. IT MADE THEM RELAX.
LET THEIR GUARD DOWN. THAT'S HOW I WAS ABLE TO TAIL THEM AND GET THE REAL STORY.

A GROUP LIKE THIS, YOU JUST KNOW THEY'RE GOING TO HAVE A SECRET HIDEOUT.
OVER ON THE SOUTH SIDE- MATILDA'S GREENHOUSE.
MATILDA IS WELL KNOWN HERE- SHE SUPPLIES RESTAURANTS LIKE CHEF'S PLACE WITH THE VERY BEST INGREDIENTS FROM HER GARDENS.
NO ONE SAW YOU, DID THEY?
AND SHE PROVIDES A PERFECT BASE OF OPERATIONS FOR THE ANGRIES TO WORK FROM.
HURRY!
IT LOOKS LIKE SHE USES SOME OF HER FOOD CHEMISTRY KNOWLEDGE TO MAKE SUPPLIES THE GROUP CAN USE IN THEIR WAR ON CRIME.
THE PLACE ISN'T OPEN TO THE PUBLIC, SO THEY HAVE PERFECT CONDITIONS TO PLOT AND PLAN.
IT'S A GREAT SETUP. I HATE TO BE THE ONE WHO CAUSES IT TO ALL GO DOWN...

BUT A RAVEN'S GOTTA EAT.
NICE NIGHT FOR A WALK, EH?
EEP! UH, YEAH.
SO WHAT'S THE DEAL HERE, WHY ARE YOU SPYING AROUND THIS NEIGHBOR-HOOD?
ARE YOU IN CAHOOTS WITH THE PIGS?
COME ON, FESS UP.
ULP!
SEE, RAY? THEY DON'T CARE HOW LEGAL YOUR REPORTER WORK IS.
THEY JUST WORRY ABOUT THEIR OWN AGENDA.
LIKE EVERYBODY ELSE HERE.
WHO'S THAT?
MY BOSS! OLD MIGHTY.

GET IN, RAY.
GLADLY.
HE'S THE PUBLISHER OF THE ***EAGLE'S EYE!***
YOU'VE GOT US ALL WRONG- WE'RE HERE TO CLEAN UP NEW YOLK!
I'VE HEARD IT ALL BEFORE, KID.
THAT'S WHAT THE PIGS SAID WHEN THEY MOVED IN.

SPEAKING OF PIGS- LOOK!
OOF-
CLANG!

OUTTA THERE, YOU LOUSY SPIES!
HEYA!
KWANG!

BETTER START SQUEALIN', PIG.
WE WEREN'T FOLLOWIN' YOU! WE WERE FOLLOWIN' THE RAVEN!
WHO... WAS FOLLOWIN' ***YOU.***

AYAYAYAYAYA
YIYIYIYIYIYIYIYIYI
NOT GOOD ENOUGH. GIVE 'EM THE PIZZA TWIRL FOR A MINUTE, THUNDERBIRD.
WHAT DO YOU KNOW?
NOTHIN'! YET.
HEH HEH.
IT LOOKS LIKE THE RAVEN FOUND OUT A TON FROM ALL THE NOTES HE'S MADE!
ALL WE GOTTA DO IS WAIT FOR TOMORROW'S PAPER TO COME OUT.
AND GET SOMEONE TO READ IT TO US!
NOT IF WE CAN CONVINCE MIGHTY -- OH.
I CAN CATCH UP TO THEM, CHASER!
IF WE FORCE THEM TO DROP THE STORY...
...THEN WE'RE AS BAD AS THE PIGS.

WHERE DID YOU ALL GO, AND WHY DO YOU ALL LOOK LIKE YOU'VE JUST LOST YOUR LAST EGG?
I JUST REMEMBERED I GOTTA-
-SIGH- MIGHT AS WELL TELL YOU NOW, 'TILD.
YOU GOTTA STAY AND FACE IT LIKE THE REST OF US.
A REPORTER FROM THE EAGLE'S EYE TRACKED US DOWN!
HE KNOWS EVERYTHING ABOUT OUR OPERATION... AND THEY'RE ABOUT TO REVEAL IT TO THE WHOLE CITY.
MAYOR HOGG WILL SEND THE COPS TO SHUT THIS PLACE DOWN AS SOON AS HE- WELL, AS SOON AS SOMEONE READS THE PAPER TO HIM.
OH, MIGHTY, YOU REALLY DON'T BELIEVE IN ANYONE ANYMORE.
MIGHTY? EAGLE?
YOU KNOW HIM?
OH, YES. WE GO WAY BACK.
WE WERE BOTH SUCCESSFUL, PROMINENT CITIZENS OF NEW YOLK. ALWAYS IN THE PAPER FOR OUR CHARITY OR EVEN JUST BEING OUT ON THE TOWN.
THOSE WERE HAPPY DAYS.

THEN HARD TIMES HAPPENED, LIKE THEY ALWAYS DO. BUSINESSES CLOSED. MIGHTY LOST EVERYTHING BUT HIS NEWSPAPER, I ONLY HAD MY GREENHOUSE LEFT.
FREE SOUP & COFFEE FOR UNEMPLOYED
ANY JOB WILL DO!
IT WAS A STRUGGLE, BUT WE STILL HAD EACH OTHER -- FOR A WHILE.
FREE SOUP
CHOPPER FOR MAYOR
VOTE PIG
BUT THE PUBLIC WAS DESPERATE AND ELECTED MAYOR HOGG, WHO PROMISED TO BRING BACK PROSPERITY. INSTEAD HE FILLED ALL THE BIG POSITIONS IN TOWN WITH HIS CORRUPT MINIONS.
AND THE KING PIG OF CRIME WAS ABLE TO MOVE HIS MOB IN WITHOUT ANY OPPOSITION.
SOUP FOR UNEMPLOYED
WE SUNK OURSELVES INTO OUR WORK TO HELP OUT IN THE ONLY WAYS WE COULD, BUT DIDN'T HAVE TIME FOR EACH OTHER.
EVENTUALLY WE DRIFTED APART.
I NEVER WANTED TO GIVE UP ON THE CITY, THAT'S WHY I WAS HAPPY TO LET YOU ALL WORK OUT OF HERE.
BUT MAYBE IT'S FINALLY TIME TO GO.
KNOCK! KNOCK!
HI. THIS...IS A MOCK-UP OF THE PAPER, IT WON'T COME OUT UNTIL MIDDAY.
THE BOSS WANTED TO GIVE YOU A HEAD START.

"A GREENHOUSE FULL OF ANGRY BIRDS."
IT'S A GOOD PICTURE OF US, AT LEAST.
THANKS.
BACK TO THAT CRUMMY FLAT BY THE DUMP, I GUESS. WHAT DO YOU WANT HELP WITH MOVING, 'TILD?
MATILDA?
CLICK
TOOK YOU LONG ENOUGH, RAY. NOW LET'S GET BACK TO WORK.

RA- SAY!
I JUST WANTED TO THANK YOU FOR GIVING US SOME TIME.
AND TO LET YOU KNOW THAT I UNDERSTAND. YOU HAVE TO PROTECT THE EAGLE'S EYE.

I KNEW I WOULDN'T BE ABLE TO GET AWAY WITH THIS OPERATION FOREVER.
BUT WHEN RED AND THE GANG CAME TO TOWN LOOKING TO FIGHT BACK...

...IT REMINDED ME OF HOW WE USED TO BE BEFORE THE CITY WORE US DOWN.
I HAD TO HELP THEM GIVE IT A SHOT.
I BETTER COLLECT MY THINGS. TAKE CARE, MIGHTY.
LATER.
THOUGHT THE COPS WOULD BE HERE BY NOW.
HUH?
EXTRA EXTRA! THE LATE EDITION IS FINALLY OUT!
HEALTH WARNING ON THE SOUTH SIDE!
WHERE'S THE PIECE ON US? THERE'S THE GREENHOUSE...
"BLOCKS AROUND THE OLD GREENHOUSE ARE HEAVY WITH TRUFFLE HERBS WHICH CAUSE VIOLENT ALLERGY REACTIONS..."
THE EAGLE'S EYE

"...TO SENSITIVE PIG SKIN. TOO HARD TO REMOVE, EXPERTS RECOMMEND ALL PIGS STAY CLEAR OF THE AREA"-
WHAT IS THIS?! WHERE'S THE BIG EXPOSÉ ON THE COSTUME BIRDS?!
THE EAGLE'S EYE
HEALTH WARNING ISSUED!
WASN'T FINDING ANYTHING, BUT THEN GOT WIND OF THIS EMERGENCY. THOUGHT IT WOULD HELP YOUR BOYS.
HE'S RIGHT, BOSS, THAT STUFF IS NASTY! I COULDN'T BREATHE OR EAT RIGHT FOR A DAY!
BAH, THANKS, I GUESS.
SNOUT, TELL OUR GUYS TO CLEAR OUT OF THE GREENHOUSE DISTRICT.
SNIFF
THE BEGINNING!

ARTWORK BY **MARCELO FERREIRA**
COLORS BY **DIEGO RODRIGUEZ**

CHAPTER TWO

ARTWORK BY RON RANDALL
COLORS BY ANTTI MERILUOTO

SUPER ANGRY BIRDS
THE NEST EGG
WEDNESDAY MORNING 8:51 AM. THE NEW YOLK TREASURY BUILDING.
BASTION OF THE NEW YOLK EGG RESERVE SYSTEM. THE EGG STANDARD... THE BASIS FOR NOT ONLY THE CITY'S ECONOMY, BUT COMMERCE THE WORLD OVER. ONE DOLLAR = ONE EGG.

THIS STANDARD LEAVES NEW YOLK ON SOLID FINANCIAL GROUNDING, ALLOWING FOR THE EXCHANGE OF ANY GOODS, BACKED BY THE VALUE OF A VAST EGG RESERVE.
9:15 AM.
CLEAREST SOUND OF ANY RADIO, SIR. YOU'VE MADE A FINE CHOICE.
9:23 AM.
PROFITS ARE UP. AGAIN.
9:46 AM.
A MICROSCOPE, ONE HUNDRED TEST TUBES, A SOLDERING IRON, ONE CARTON OF NITROGLYCERINE, TWENTY FEET OF COPPER WIRE.
THANKS FOR COMING TO MAD SCIENTIST SUPPLIES. IT'S ALWAYS SO GOOD TO SEE YOU, PROFESSOR PIG.

9:51 AM.
SORRY IT'S ALL IN CHANGE.
DOESN'T MATTER, BOYS. IT'S ALL MONEY.
10:07 AM.
SOON, ALL THE PROFITS WILL BE OURS. AND NO ONE SUSPECTS A THING.
10:15 AM.
CAN YOU BELIEVE THESE STORIES ABOUT THE SUPER ANGRY BIRDS? CAN THEY BE REAL?
PRODUCE
EGGCITEMENT!!!
REAL MAD, BUT... REAL?
10:22 AM.
I THINK YOU'LL FIND IT'S ALL THERE.
10:27 AM.
YOU SURE DO GO THROUGH A LOT OF SHOES, SIR.
UHH, YEAH. I DO A LOT OF RUNNING.
THLETIC.
Women's

10:30 AM.
CLIKK
!!!
LOOK OUT!
SLAMMMMMM!
OH!

DID YOU SEE THAT?
AN ACCIDENT?
IS EVERYBODY OKAY?
WHAT HAPPENED?
DANG, THERE'S EGGS ALL OVER.
OH, SIR. I'M SO SORRY. THIS... THIS IS...
HEY, NO PROBLEM. THIS WAS, ERR, TOTALLY MY FAULT.

HUH? BUT... BUT I RAN THE RED LIGHT. I'M SO SORRY THAT...
NOT A PROBLEM... THESE THINGS HAPPEN.
LET'S NOT WORRY ABOUT WHO SHOULD BE BLAMED.
YOU RECOGNIZE THOSE DRIVERS?
YEAH. TWO OF KINGPIG'S THUGS. WHAT ARE THEY DOING DRIVING AN ARMORED CAR?
THIS COULD GET UGLY, RED.
THIS IS ALREADY UGLY, CHASER.
LET'S KICK SOME #&^@!
HERE'S MY INSURANCE INFORMATION SO THAT...
WON'T BE NECESSARY. MY COMPANY WILL COVER ALL DAMAGES. JUST SEND US A BILL.
YOU HEARING THIS?
YEAH. STRANGE.

10:43 AM.
ERRRRRT!
SQUEEKY CLEAN
"I'VE NEVER SEEN A PIG ACT SO NICE."
STAY BACK, EVERYONE. STAY BACK.
WE'LL GET THIS SORTED OUT.
SQUEEKY CLEAN
THANK YOU, EVERYONE. THANKS SO MUCH.
THOSE MEN LOOK AWFULLY FAMILIAR.
I'M SURPRISED YOU DON'T RECOGNIZE THEM RIGHT OFF.
WAIT A SECOND. ARE THOSE...?
"YEAH. EVEN MORE OF KINGPIG'S MEN. BUT WHAT ARE THEY DOING HERE?"
ARE YOU OKAY? NEED ANY MEDICAL AID?
NO... NO SIR.
GOOD. GOOD. WE'LL GET THIS CLEANED UP AND YOU CAN GO ON YOUR WAY.

WE'LL PAY FOR ALL DAMAGES OF COURSE.
YES. THE OTHER MAN SAID THAT, BUT, IT WAS MY FAULT AND I...
YOU GET THAT CLEANED UP BACK THERE?
ALL CLEAN!
AND DISINFECTED!
GOOD. EXCELLENT. LOOKS LIKE WE'RE DONE HERE. HERE'S SOME MONEY. SORRY YOU WERE INCONVENIENCED.
BUT I...
10:48 AM.
OH.
ZOOOOOOM!
WHOOOOSH!
WELL, THAT WAS ODD. THE KINGPIG'S MEN ARE USUALLY INCREDIBLY AGGRESSIVE, BUT THEY WERE... NICE.
YEAH. AND THEY NEVER TAKE THE BLAME FOR ANYTHING, BUT THIS TIME THEY WERE APOLOGIZING. AND THAT CLEANUP WAS SO QUICK.
A PIG CLEANING UP AND APOLOGIZING? SOMETHING'S WRONG.

IT'S LIKE IT NEVER EVEN HAPPENED.
THEY DID A GREAT JOB OF CLEANING, THAT'S FOR SURE.
YOU... YOU'RE THE SUPER ANGRY BIRDS!
HMM. MISSED A SPOT, HERE.
LOOKS LIKE A BIT OF...
...EGG?
-SNIFF-
-SNIFF-
PECK
PECK
HMMM...
MADE OF PEWTER.
THOSE EGGS WERE FAKE.

11:38 AM.
SO... DO YOU THINK THE ENTIRE SHIPMENT OF EGGS WAS FAKE?
IT'S LIKELY. WHERE THERE'S ONE ROTTEN EGG, THERE'S USUALLY ANOTHER.
BUT THOSE EGGS WERE BOUND FOR THE RESERVE.
I KNOW. THIS COULD BE BAD.
AND WHAT DID THE KINGPIG'S MEN HAVE TO DO WITH IT?
ARGGH! THAT'S WHAT I DON'T KNOW. BUT I'M GOING TO FIND OUT. HOPEFULLY BY SMACKING SOME HEADS AROUND.
KRAKKK!
SO... WE NEED A PLAN.
I'VE GOT ONE.
DOES IT INVOLVE DANGER? CONSTANT THREAT? LIVES TOTTERING ON THE PRECIPICE? BLOWING UP SOME PIGS AND CAUSING MASSIVE DAMAGE?
YEAH. THAT'S PRETTY MUCH MY PLAN.
THEN I'M IN.

12:41 PM. THE GENTLEMAN PIG (OWNED AND OPERATED BY CHEF PIG).
Matilda's
WHO'S THIS GUY?
MY NEW HELPER.
CHEF PIG HAS BEEN ORDERING MORE AND MORE FLOWERS TO MAKE THE RESTAURANT LOOK FESTIVE, AND I CAN'T DELIVER ALL THESE FLOWERS ALONE.
OKAY, MATILDA. GO ON IN.
12:58 PM.
FWUMPP
---PEWTER---
---SHIPMENT---
---THROTTLE---

1:07 PM.

HMMM. VERY INTERESTING.

CLIKK
1:08 PM.
CLIKK

WELLLL...

1:41 PM. THE TRAIN YARDS.
YOU GUYS GOT A LOTTA NERVE!
SO... WE'RE GOING TO BE ASKING YOU GUYS SOME QUESTIONS.
AND WE WON'T BE TELLING YOU ANYTHING.
I RESPECT THAT. I REALLY DO.
I MEAN, SECRETS ARE SUPPOSED TO BE HIDDEN.
LIKE, HIDDEN BEHIND A BRICK WALL FOR INSTANCE.
LIKE... THIS BRICK WALL HERE.
SMAASSHH!
NOW, I FIND MYSELF WONDERING... WHERE ARE YOUR SECRETS HIDING?

1:53 PM. HAMHATTAN BANK.
1:53 PM.
1:53 PM.
1:53 PM.
RECORDS
1:53 PM.
1:53 PM.

2:41 PM.
SLAMMM!
SO NOW WE KNOW.
"KINGPIG HAS BEEN SECRETLY REPLACING ALL OF NEW YOLK'S EGG RESERVES WITH FAKE EGGS.
"IT'S WIDESPREAD ENOUGH THAT THE ENTIRE CITY COULD GO BANKRUPT.
"AND THE KINGPIG WOULD HAVE ALL THE REAL RICHES."
UNFORTUNATELY, WE DON'T HAVE ANY IDEA OF WHERE THE COUNTERFEITERS ARE WORKING FROM, OR WHERE THE REAL EGGS ARE BEING KEPT.
YEAH, THEY'RE REALLY GUARDING THEIR *#%@ SECRETS, FOR ONCE!
DON'T WORRY, GUYS...

"I HAVE A PLAN."
4:14 PM.
KRRR-WHUMPPFF!
WHA...? GAHHH!
OINK OINK! SNORT SNORT!
WHAT JUST HAPPENED?
NOT SURE. SOMETHING HIT US.
LET KINGPIG KNOW SOMETHING'S HAPPENING! AND LET'S GET SOME MORE MEN HERE!
ARMORED EGGBASKET
WE CAN'T TAKE ANY CHANCES WITH THIS SHIPMENT WE'RE...

ALL MEN! CLOSE IN! WE ARE UNDER ATTACK! REPEAT... WE ARE UNDER ATTACK!
OH NO.
P-KOW!
BANG!
BANG!
P-KOW!
K-TWEEEN
IT'S NOT HAVING ANY EFFECT!
UNHHH!
WHAMMMMMMM!
4:16 PM.
GOT HIM!
HE'S STILL MOVING!
POUR IT ON, BOYS! POUR IT ON!

4:17 PM.
CRUNNCH!
HELLO, PIGGIES.
GAHHH!
THERE'S ANOTHER ONE OVER THERE!
IT'S THOSE BIRDS!
TAKE HIM DOWN! RUSH HIM!
RUSH HIM? HAH! WRONG MOVE, BOYS.
YOU SHOULD ALWAYS WALK SOFTLY...
...WHEN THERE'S A BOMB AROUND.
ARGHH!
FFF-WHUMMPPP!
GAHH!
GUHH!
4:18 PM.
ERRRRRRRT

YOU'RE NO MATCH FOR THOSE FREAKIN' BIRDS! GET IN THE ARMORED CAR!
LET'S GET OUT OF HERE! HURRY! HURRY!
POLICE
A COP? DID KINGPIG SEND YOU?
WHO ELSE? WE CAN'T LET THIS SHIPMENT GET STOLEN BY THE SUPER ANGRY BIRDS!
LET THOSE GUYS BACK THERE DEAL WITH THE BIRDS WHILE WE...
FLOOR IT!
SCREEECH!
4:27 PM.
WHEW. THAT WAS CLOSE.
6

YOU SAVED US, DUDE.
COMPLETELY SAVED US. THOSE BIRDS WERE GOING TO TEAR US APART.
SAVE YOUR THANKS.
A STUNT LIKE THIS COULD COST ME MY JOB.
THE KINGPIG OWES ME. OWES ME BIG.
HAH! MONEY'S FREE THESE DAYS. WE'RE MAKING IT OURSELVES!
NO PROBLEM THERE!
HA HA! I GUESS THAT'S TRUE!
SHOULD WE HEAD BACK TO THE HIDEOUT?
YEAH. BEST CHECK IN.
HOLD ON A SECOND.
NOW THAT WE'VE LOST THOSE BIRDS, I WANT TO CHECK ON SOMETHING.

4:46 PM.
WHY'D WE STOP?
I THOUGHT I HEARD A NOISE. I'M WORRIED THUNDER-BIRD DAMAGED THE TRUCK TOO MUCH TO DRIVE.
LOOKS FINE, THOUGH. LET'S GET ROLLING.
I'M TIRED OF DRIVING. ONE OF YOU TAKE THE WHEEL.
NO PROBLEM. I LOVE DRIVING.
YOU JUST LIKE BEING IN CHARGE.
YEAH. AND I GET TO HONK THE HORN, AND SCARE OTHER CARS.
HONNNNNK!
5:03 PM.
HA HA HA HA HA!
HA HA OINK OINK HA HA HA!

5:29 PM.
WE'RE HERE.
SO THIS IS WHERE ALL THE COUNTERFEIT EGGS ARE MADE?
YEP. AND THE REAL EGGS ARE STORED HERE, TOO, ONCE WE SWAP THEM OUT.
HEY. WAIT A MINUTE. HOW COME YOU DIDN'T KNOW THAT?
YEAH? AIN'T YOU ONE OF US?
ONE OF YOU? NEVER. ALTHOUGH YOU MIGHT SAY...
...THAT I AM INDEED...
...A COUNTERFEIT.
CHASER!!!

12:32 AM.
STUNNING NEWS TODAY, WHEN AN IMMENSE COUNTERFEITING RING THAT COULD HAVE SHAKEN NEW YOLK'S FOUNDATIONS WAS SMASHED BY THE SUPER ANGRY BIRDS.
CAN'T SLEEP, RED?
NO. NO I CAN'T.
12:34 AM.
BUT AT LEAST THE CITY CAN.
HMMM. THE SUPER ANGRY BIRDS. I CAN'T TAKE THIS ANYMORE.
THEY'VE BEEN A THORN IN MY SIDE FOR TOO LONG, AND NOW THEY DESTROY MY COUNTERFEITING OPERATION?
WELL THEN, YOU'VE JUST STARTED A WAR.
FOR REAL.
THE END

ARTWORK BY **MARCELO FERREIRA**
COLORS BY **DIEGO RODRIGUEZ**

CHAPTER THREE

ARTWORK BY RON RANDALL
COLORS BY ANTTI MERILUOTO

ADD THE YEAST, KNEAD THE DOUGH, INTO THE BIG HOT OVEN YOU GO--
--WHEN YOU RISE, SO DELICIOUS--
--SURE TO GRANT EVERYONE'S WISHES?
HAWMP
CHOMP CHOMP
SAYYY! STOP! YOU GOTTA PAY FOR THAT!
MMM! CREAM FILLING!
YOU'RE THE NEW BUSINESS HERE, SO YOU DON'T KNOW HOW THINGS WORK. LEMME ENLIGHTEN YEZ.
WE'RE KINGPIG'S GANG-- WE DON'T PAY FOR NOTHIN'!
OPEN
THAT BAKER NEEDS HELP-- SUPER HELP!
SUPER ANGRY BIRDS
THE BIRD BUSTER

I'M STILL HUNGRY! BAKE UP SOME MORE OF THOSE TWISTY THINGS.
NO! I WORKED HARD TO START MY OWN BAKERY AND I'M NOT ROLLING OVER FOR A BUNCHA GANGSTERS!
OF COURSE, POPS. YOU DON'T GOTTA LIFT A FINGER!
I'LL BAKE UP SOMETHIN' MYSELF.
NO!
WONDER HOW LONG IT'LL TAKE THIS TO RISE?
YOU WIN, PAL!
YA CAN TELL EVERYBODY YA RAN US OUTTA YOUR SHOP-- HEE HEE!
CAN'T LET IT BE DESTROYED-- BUT--
FFSSSSSSHH
I MUST LIVE TO BAKE AGAIN!
OPEN

KABOOOM
OFFICER! THAT GANG DESTROYED MY SHOP!
QUIET YOU, IT'S NEW COMICS DAY.
HA, ALMOST FORGOT THE TIP JAR!
SO YA HAD TO LEARN THE HARD WAY HOW BUSINESS WORKS HERE IN NEW YOLK CITY. WE'RE THE GANGS AND THE POLICE.
EVERYTHING THAT HAPPENS HERE IS BECAUSE THE PIG GANG ALLOWS IT TO HAPPEN.
TOUGH LESSON, BAKER. JUST BE GLAD YER STILL BREATHIN'.
EXCUSE ME, MR. CRIMINAL HOG GUY?
THERE'S SOME FOLKS HERE WHO SAY THEY HAVE ANOTHER LESSON-- THIS TIME FOR YOU!

WHO JUST BLEW SOMETHING UP? THAT'S MY CALLING CARD!
IT WAS THE NEW BAKERY, AND I DIDN'T EVEN GET TO TRY THEIR CINNAMON ROLLS YET!
YOU GANGSTERS WANT TO TRY PUSHING US AROUND?
NEVER MIND, I CAN'T WAIT FOR AN ANSWER. SUPER ANGRY BIRDS...
...LAUNCH!

RA-BAMM
SPLAKT
LET'S GO--
--FOR A--
--SPIN!
A-A-A-A-A-I-I-I-I-I--
OH, LIKE TO PLAY WITH EXPLOSIVES, HAH?
LEMME SHOW YOU WHY THEY CALL ME THE BOMB!
BOOOMM

"AND THEN I DON'T REMEMBER MUCH AFTER THAT, BOSS..."
...THOSE BIRDS JUST HAVE TOO MUCH FIREPOWER!
AND THEY'RE STRONG.
AND FAST! IT'S A REAL POWER IMBALANCE, I THINK YA CALL IT.
I'M SICKA THOSE BIRDS! THIS IS THE LAST TIME THEY HAND MY GUYS THEIR HATS.
PERFESSER! YOU BETTER BE THROUGH WITH THAT CONTRAPTION!
INDEED I AM, KINGPIG!
ONE MORE CALIBRATION AND THIS WILL BE READY FOR OPERATION.
NICE. OKAY, BOYS, GET BACK OUT IN BIRD TERRITORY.
YOU'RE GONNA BE *BAIT*.

THE NEXT DAY!
OVER HERE, HURRY!
LET ME AT THEM!
THA BOIDS ARE HERE!
ABOUT TIME! WE'VE BEEN SHAKIN' THIS GUY DOWN SINCE BREAKFAST.
YOU PIGS ARE REAL GLUTTONS FOR PUNISHMENT, HUH?
YEAH, YOU COULD SAY THAT.
AND HERE COMES THE PUNISHER.
FOR YOU.
CLOMP CLOMP CLOMP CLOMP CLOMP CLOMP CLOMP CLOMP CLOMP
UH, WHAT THE HECK?
IS IT A CAR?

SUPER BIRDS IDENTIFIED.
RED RAMMER: SUPERIOR TARGETING AND RAMMING POWER.
CHASER: UNNATURALLY HIGH SPEEDS.
THUNDER-BIRD: GREAT STRENGTH.
BOMB: GENERATES EXPLOSIVE FORCE.
NOT A CAR, FOR YOU GUYS, IT'S MORE LIKE THE PAIN TRAIN!
IT'S A ROBOT BIRD BUSTER!
SO STEP UP, BIRDS... AND GET BUSTED UP!
BIRD BUSTER: I AM ENGINEERED TO COUNTER EACH OF THE COSTUMED BIRD'S POWERS...
...AND CRUSH THEM.

I THINK WE NEED TO SEND THIS HUNK O' JUNK TO THE CRUSHER.
THUNDERBIRD, FLATTEN THAT BIG TOY!
DEPLOY--
HNNH!

NNH!
AVOID-- PUNCH.

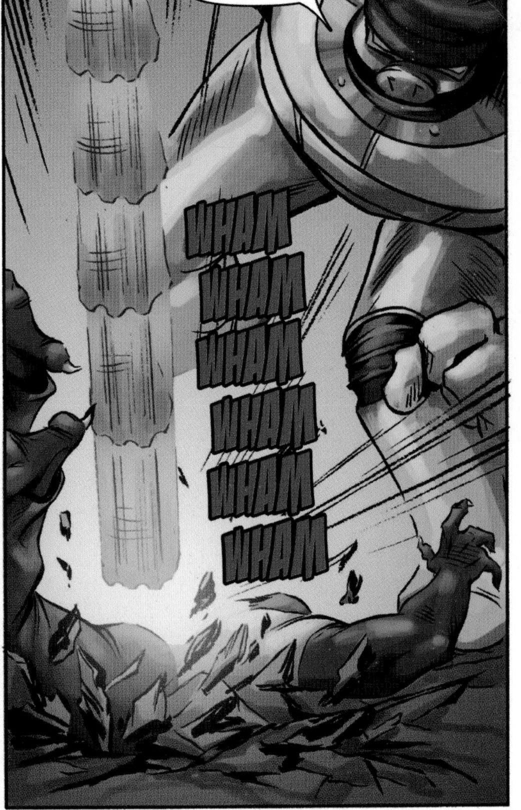
--JACK-HAMMER.
WHAM WHAM WHAM WHAM WHAM WHAM

NO ONE DOES THAT TO--
--THUNDERBIRD!
BANNNG
EVERY STRUCTURE HAS--
--A WEAK SPOT!
BONNNG
RAMMER BIRD-- VERY PERSISTENT.
SOLUTION--
--EJECTION.
HEEEEEEYYYYYYYYYYYYYYY--

WOW, THIS THING IS PRETTY EFFICIENT!
THE PIGS HAVE SOME SERIOUS BRAIN WORKING FOR THEM.
BUT THIS BRUTE WILL STILL HAVE TO PLAY CATCH UP!
CHASER BIRD IN MOTION...
I'M GONNA TAKE YOU APART BEFORE YOU CAN LAY A FOOT ON ME!
SPEED: 88 MPH
CALCULATE SPEED-- PREDICT PATH--
--INTERCEPT.
ZZAAAKT
YA-A-A-A-A-A-AAAAA

THAT'S ENOUGH, YOU!
CALL THE SCRAP TRUCK, JAKE--THEY'LL NEED TO HAUL OFF SOME METAL!
PREPARE FOR EXPLOSIVE DISCHARGE.
ZZSSHH
IMPLEMENT--
WHOOOM
--FORCE DOME.
HA! GOOD DEMONSTRATION, BUSTER. TIME TA REPORT IN.

SOON!
EXTRA, EXTRA! THE BIRDS FACE A NEW CHALLENGE!
ROBOT PIG ON A RAMPAGE!
THE EAGLE'S EYE
SORRY RED-- WE STILL GOTTA SELL PAPERS!
GIVE ME THAT! THE NEWS IS SAYING WE'RE WASHED UP?
I DON'T GET IT... THE PIGS ARE TOO STUPID TO PUT SOMETHING LIKE THIS TOGETHER.
THEY'VE GOT SOME SCIENTIST WORKING FOR THEM, FROM WHAT I'VE HEARD.
EVERY THING MADE HAS A WEAK POINT. WE JUST HAVE TO KEEP TESTING.
NEW ATTACKS, APPROACHES...
HEY, ANGRIES!
I THINK YOU'LL GET YOUR CHANCE, THERE'S PIGS BEIN' JERKS OVER AT POPPINJAY PARK!
LET'S GO, BOYS!

OH MY--!
BAW!
POP!
WATCH WHERE YER GOIN' LADY.
GOTCHA MA'AM!
URK.
YOU GUYS ACT PRETTY SMUG CONSIDERING YOUR TOY SOLDIER ISN'T AROUND.
OH, HE'S ALWAYS AROUND, BIRDIE.
LOOK UP!
OKAY, GUYS, ROUND TWO!

I'M GONNA BLAST THROUGH THAT FORCE-FIELD THIS TIME!
EXPLOSIVE BIRD ON APPROACH AT FULL INTENSITY.
PROJECT FORCE DOME LATERAL-OUTWARD--
HUH--
BAWHOOOM

NOW HE'S MAKING *US* WRECK THE PARK INSTEAD OF HIM!
OKAY, THIS TIME, I'LL RAM HIM AND DISTRACT HIM, WHILE YOU RUN AROUND BEHIND AND TRY TO FIND AN ACCESS PANEL TO--
ZZAAAP
ZZZAAAP
OH, GOSH, SORRY YA DIDN'T GET TO FINISH, RED RAMMER! HAW!
WHY DON'TCHA GO SLEEP IT OFF?
COME BACK WHEN YA FEEL LIKE GETTING STOMPED AGAIN!
FACE IT, YOU BIRDS ARE WASHED UP IN THIS TOWN!

YOU POOR BOYS! MAYBE YOU SHOULD TAKE A BREAK FROM BATTLING THIS MACHINE.
NOT WHEN WE'RE... SO CLOSE. UGH.
BOY, I WAS SURE WE'D TAKE THAT BRUISER APART BY NOW.
I FEEL LIKE IT'S ME WHO'S BEING TAKEN APART.
IT'S DESIGNED PERFECTLY TO TAKE YOU ON, IS THE PROBLEM.
AND IT DOESN'T HOLD BACK, IT LETS US HAVE IT WITH EVERYTHING IT'S GOT.
BUT WE CAN'T DO THAT. IF I JUST KEPT BOMBING THE THING, I'D LEVEL THE TOWN!
YEAH...
...WE'RE HOLDING BACK...
JIM, YOU DELIVER THE NEWS-- GO GIVE THE PIGS *THIS* NEWS.
"THEY SAY THEY'RE GONNA MEET HERE?"

THOSE BIRDS WOULDN'T DARE FACE US RIGHT AT THE STATION!
I THINK THE ROBOT'S BRAINED 'EM SO MUCH THEY'RE GETTIN' PUNCHY IN THE HEAD.
IT'S SOME KINDA TRICK TA DISTRACT US.
NO TRICK!
SAY!
WE WOULDN'T WANT TO CATCH YA WITH YOUR PANTS DOWN.
IN HOT PURSUIT.
GET THOSE HOODLUMS!
THAT'S RIGHT, BIG BOY.
CATCH ME IF YOU CAN!
HEY, NO! NOT THERE--
KSMASSH

PHBBLLLTHH!
LOOK, BOLTS, THAT BIRD IS DISRESPECTING YOUR AUTHORITY!
SURRENDER.
THE MACHINE IS ONTO US, GUYS!
WHUNCH
BUST THOSE BIRDS! THEY BROKE MY POLICE STATION!
I KNOW A NICE HOUSE WHERE WE CAN HIDE OUT!
WHY, I BELIEVE THIS IS THE HOME OF THE KING PIG OF CRIME!
CLANG!
GOOD PUNCH, THUNDERBIRD.

WOW, GOOD ONE, ROBOT!
THAT'LL SEND OUR GUY RIGHT THROUGH THE SECOND STORY...
WHAMM
"...LOOKS LIKE SOMEBODY'S BEDROOM."
HOINK!!!
IN HOT PURSUIT.
EXCUSE ME.
WHAT IS ALL DIS!!?!
CRASH
EVERYBODY TAKE COVER--
--PUT OUT ANY FIRES BEFORE THEY GET BIG!
BLUB!

WILL--
EXTERMINATE--
BIRDS--
HE'S GOT US ON THE ROPES!
HOW LONG WILL WE LAST?
LONGER THAN THIS MANSION I BET!
THE BIRD BUSTER IS PROVING MOST EFFECTIVE.
HE'S EFFECTIVELY DESTROYIN' MY HOME! SHUT 'IM DOWN!
SHUTDOWN MODE! NOW I NEED A FEW HOURS TO REPROGRAM HIM TO STAY AWAY FROM KEY AREAS...
POW-ERRINNNNG DOWWWWWNN...
CRASH
BOOM
LEAVE SOME OF IT, I KNOW ANOTHER USE FOR THIS THING!

BAKERY
HOPPY'S
BACK IN BUSINESS
SO I SAW THE GUY WHO MUST HAVE BUILT THE ROBOT, HE DIDN'T SEEM LIKE AN ORDINARY PIG.
I GUESS IT'S POSSIBLE THEY CAN'T ALL BE BAD.
THAT PROFESSOR GUY SEEMED LIKE HE WAS WORKING AGAINST HIS WILL, WE NEED TO FIND OUT MORE ABOUT HIM.
THIS IS ON THE HOUSE GENTS!
AW, YOU STILL HAD TO MAKE REPAIRS, WE DON'T MIND PAYING.
YES, BUT I'LL BE BACK IN THE BLACK SOON ENOUGH...
...THIS NEW OVEN WORKS EVEN BETTER THAN MY FIRST ONE!
DING! CROISSANTS ARE READY--
THE END

ARTWORK BY MARCELO FERREIRA
COLORS BY DIEGO RODRIGUEZ

CHAPTER FOUR

ARTWORK BY RON RANDALL
COLORS BY ANTTI MERILUOTO

The REAL EGG
HEY! YOU KIDS!
KINGPIG DON'T NEED NO BRATS 'ROUND HERE.
Kit Kat Club
RUN!
SUPER ANGRY BIRDS
STELLA SINGS THE BLUES

GO! GO! GO!
RAWRRFF
RAWRRFF
RAWRRFF

HMMM?

LET ME TELL YOU A STORY
OF A MAN GONE WRONG
THERE'S THAT VOICE AGAIN.
HER VOICE IS SO BEAUTIFUL. HAUNTING.
SERIOUSLY, THOUGH, DID WE OUTRUN THE DOGS?
LET ME SING YOU A STORY
OF A MAN DONE BAD
SHHH. LISTEN TO ***THAT.*** IT'S THE SAME MUSIC FROM THE NIGHT BEFORE, WHEN WE...
LET OTHERS SPEAK OF
RAINBOWS AND BIRDSONG
HA HA HA HA HA!
"...WERE MAKING SURE KINGPIG'S MEN WOULDN'T BE ABLE TO PICK HIM UP ON TIME.
"REMEMBER? HE WAS STRANDED AFTER THAT OPERA?
THIS SONG'S ABOUT
A GIRL GONE SAD
"AND THE NIGHT AFTER THAT, AFTER KINGPIG'S MEN STOLE THE MONEY WE MADE SELLING NEWSPAPERS, AND..."

"...WHEN WE WERE STEALING THE MONEY BACK, AND WE HEARD THE VOICE.
MAN DONE BAD.
MAN DONE WRONG.
"AND THEN AFTER WE STOLE KINGPIG'S COAT FROM THE KIT KAT CLUB, THAT NIGHT...
"...A COUPLE HOURS LATER, WE HEARD THE VOICE AGAIN."
GIRL GONE SAD.
WOMAN SINGS SONG
IT'S HOW THIS STORY'S TOLD...
SO BEAUTIFUL.
...AND IF I MIGHT BE SO BOLD...

...I THINK YOU'RE THE MAN
WHO ENJOYS DOING WRONG.
I THINK IT'S TIME TO SOLVE THIS MYSTERY. I THINK IT'S COMING FROM THIS WAY.
LA LA LA HMM HMM LA LA LA
AND ALONG THIS LEDGE.
HERE. OVER THIS FENCE.
HMM HMM LA LA LA HMM HMM
LA LA HOO LA LA
OVER HERE, GUYS! LOOK...
BOO LA LA BOO HOO
IT'S STELLA.
WHY OH WHY DOES A GIRL
LOVE A BAD BAD MAN?

"HUH? THAT HATCHECK GIRL FROM THE KIT KAT CLUB?
"SHE'S THE ONE WHO ALWAYS GIVES US AN EXTRA QUARTER WHENEVER SHE BUYS A PAPER."
I COULD LISTEN TO HER ALL NIGHT.
CRAZY LOVE IS ALL I SEEM TO KNOW"
IT'S A CRAZY THING, THIS CRAZY LOVE
ALL I KNOW IS CRAZY... CRAZY LOVE
UP HERE.

THIS IS THE PLACE.
YEAH. RADMI'S INDONESIAN CUISINE. ONE OF MY FAVORITE RESTAURANTS.
RADMI SAYS THAT THE KINGPIG'S MEN HAVE BEEN TRYING TO SHAKE HIM DOWN. RUN HIM OUT OF BUSINESS.
THINK HE MIGHT TRY TO BURN HIM OUT?
DOUBT IT. I THINK KINGPIG WOULD LIKE TO TAKE OVER THE BUSINESS. A FIRE DOESN'T PLAY INTO HIS PLANS.
BUT A FEW BROKEN LIMBS DO.
ERRRRT!
SO... A COUPLE WAITERS WITH BROKEN LEGS? A CHEF WITH BROKEN ARMS? RADMI IN THE HOSPITAL, MAYBE IN A COMA? THAT'S WHAT YOU'RE THINKING?
YEAH, I THINK A FEW BROKEN LIMBS ARE DEFINITELY THE KINGPIG'S PLAN. LUCKILY...
...THAT'S IN MY PLANS, TOO.

EXCUSE ME. DON'T MEAN TO TELL YOU YOUR BUSINESS, BUT...
...LOOK OUT BEHIND YOU.
YEAH. LIKE I'M GOING TO FALL FOR...
...THAT.
WHOOSH
SMAKK
UNHHH!
SMAKK
WHOOSH
NOW!!! LET'S TAKE THESE JERKS DOWN!!!
HEY, WAKE UP! SOMETHING'S GOING ON.
HUHNN?
IT'S THE SUPER ANGRY BIRDS! WOW!
GET HIM!
SMAKK
HERE'S A MESSAGE FROM THE KINGPIG!
TAKE HIM DOWN!
THUD
WHAP

THUMPP!
THUDD!
WHOA!
HOT DANG! I DON'T THINK I'VE EVER SEEN ANYBODY HIT HARDER THAN THAT!
TELL THE KINGPIG HE DOESN'T OWN THIS TOWN ANYMORE!
TELL HIM THAT, ONE DAY SOON, HE WON'T OWN ANYTHING!
RUN! HE'S GETTING READY TO--
KRAKKA-KA-KOOOOM!
HOT... SUPER... DANG!!!
OKAY, I KNOW I'VE NEVER SEEN ANYBODY HIT THAT HARD BEFORE.
C'MON. WE BETTER GET OUT OF HERE.
YEAH! WE'VE GOT PAPERS TO SELL!

SOON...
EXTRA! EXTRA! PAPER! GET'CHER PAPER! WAVE OF ASSAULTS IN NEW YOLK CITY. PROBLEM, OR... SOLUTION?
EXTRA! EXTRA! PAPER! GET'CHER PAPER!
KINGPIG'S MEN INVOLVED IN STREET BRAWLS! AND WHO ARE THE SUPER ANGRY BIRDS?
I'LL TAKE ONE!
HERE! ME!
I THINK THE SUPER ANGRY BIRDS ARE HEROES!
NO! VIGILANTES SOLVE NOTHING!
WHO CARES? WHAT ARE THE SPORTS RESULTS?
TRADITIONAL VALUES! PEACE ON THE STREETS!
I'LL TAKE A PAPER.
STELLA!
THERE YOU ARE!
WE'VE BEEN WANTING TO TALK WITH YOU!
HUH? ABOUT WHAT?
WE HEARD YOU SINGING!
-GASP-

WHY DO YOU ONLY SING IN SECRET? YOU COULD BE A STAR!
YOU SHOULD SING IN A NIGHTCLUB!
A NIGHTCLUB? NO WAY.
WHY NOT?
"BECAUSE THE KIT KAT CLUB IS OWNED BY STAG HAWG. ONE OF KINGPIG'S MEN.
"AND SASSY'S AND EL DIABLO ARE OWNED BY STAYKIN EGGS. HE'S ANOTHER OF KINGPIG'S MEN."
AND THE GOLDEN HALO, DARK HAMM'S, AND THE MAGIC GARDENS, THEY'RE ALL UNDER THE OWNERSHIP OF BUFF HEY.
ONE OF KINGPIG'S MEN?
THAT'S RIGHT. ALL OF THE NIGHTCLUBS IN NEW YOLK CITY... THEY'RE ALL OWNED BY THE KINGPIG, OR ONE OF KINGPIG'S MEN.
AND SO I WON'T SING IN ANY OF THEM.

EXTRA! EXTRA!
LISTEN UP!
WE HAVE TO DO SOMETHING ABOUT THIS.
AND SO...
YOU SEE 'EM?
NOPE.
YOU SEE 'EM?
NOPE.
YOU SEE 'EM?
NOPE.

YOU SEE 'EM?
NOPE.
YOU SEE 'EM?
NOPE.
THESE ARE KINGPIG'S MEN.
AND THE BRUISES ARE FRESH.
THEY MUST BE AROUND HERE.
UHH...
LOOK! TRACKS!
LOOKS LIKE HE WENT THROUGH HERE.
OH.
HI.
EXCUSE ME.
WE HAVE A FAVOR TO ASK.

TWELVE HOURS LATER...
HUFF
HUFF
HUFF
SNORT
BOSS! WE, UHH, HAVE A PROBLEM.
I DON'T LIKE PROBLEMS.
AND I DON'T LIKE TELLIN' THEM TO YOU, BECAUSE I KNOW YOU DON'T LIKE 'EM, BUT...
"...THAT RAMROD GUY, HE ATTACKED THE GOLDEN HALO!"
ERRRGH! LET'S SEE HOW YOU GUYS LIKE BEING BULLIED!
AHHH!
LOOK OUT!
"AND HE WAS ANGRY. LIKE... SUPER ANGRY."
AND THERE JUST WASN'T SUPER ANYTHING OUR MEN COULD DO ABOUT IT. WE LOST THE CLUB.

BOSS! WE GOT A PROBLEM!
"THAT SUPER ANGRY BIRD, BOMB! HE ATTACKED SASSY'S! HE WAS YELLING ABOUT HOW THERE NEEDS TO BE A CHANGE, ABOUT SOME DAME THAT WANTS TO SING AT NIGHTCLUBS, BUT WON'T SING AT ANY CLUB OF YOURS!
"AND... I'M SORRY, BUT... WE LOST THE CLUB."
KAAA-WHUMMMPF
I FIND THAT I AM NOT PLEASED WITH THESE REPORTS. I EXPECT MORE FROM--
BOSS! WE GOT A PROBLEM! IT WAS CHASER! THAT SUPER ANGRY BIRD!
"HE ATTACKED THE STARS CABARET! HE WAS TALKING ABOUT SOME HATCHECK GIRL THAT WANTS TO SING! HE WAS EVERYWHERE! WE DIDN'T STAND A CHANCE AGAINST HIM!"

THE CLUB WAS DESTROYED.
YOU PIGS DISAPPOINT ME.
BOSS! I'M SORRY! IF YOU COULD HAVE SEEN WHAT--
DID EVERYTHING WE COULD TO--
IF WE HAD A FEW MORE MEN, WE COULD HAVE--
SILENCE!
DO I PAY YOU TO COME TO ME WITH PROBLEMS, OR TO SOLVE PROBLEMS FOR ME?
TAKE YOUR MEN TO THE KIT KAT CLUB. IT'S MY PREMIERE CLUB. IF I LOSE THAT CLUB, I LOSE FACE.
BRING IN HAMM FIST, THE BERKSHIRE POUNDER, KID CLOBBER, AND MR. TOMBSTONE, AND ALL MY OTHER HEAVIEST HEAVIES.
I WANT THIS PROBLEM SOLVED, OR ELSE I...
...WILL SOLVE YOU. IS MY MEANING CLEAR?
CRYSTAL CLEAR, BOSS.
WE'RE SORRY. I'LL BRING IN THE BOYS, SIR.
WE'LL GET THIS FIXED.

LET'S GET OUT OF HERE!
HURRY! GO!
BEFORE HE MAKES US... DISAPPEAR.
INCOMPETENTS. I'M SURROUNDED BY INCOMPETENT FOOLS.
EHH?
ALL I KNOW IS CRAZY...
CRAZY LOVE
YOU GO PLAIN CRAZY,
WITH A CRAZY LOVE
BUT IT'S WORSE, YOU KNOW,
WITHOUT A CRAZY LOVE
CRAZY LOVE HAS ME
CRAZY IN LOVE.
THE HATCHECK GIRL.
LOVE HAS ME
CRAZY, MY LOVE,
MY CRAZY LOVE.

ELSEWHERE...
OKAY, WE'RE ON STANDBY. IF THE SUPER ANGRY BIRDS ATTACK THE KIT KAT CLUB, STAG HAWG WILL CALL THE BOSS...
...AND THE BOSS WILL CALL US, AND WE'LL GO PUT AN END TO ALL THIS GARBAGE.
NEARBY...
Kit Kat Club
KAA-BOOOOM!
UNHH!
CALL KINGPIG! GET THOSE MEN HERE! IT'S THE SUPER ANGRY BIRDS!
AHHH!
KERR-RASSHH!
THIS IS STAG HAWG! GET ME THE BOSS!

RING
RING

RING
RING
LA LA CRAAAZY LOVE LA LA.

RING
RING
CRAAAZY LA LA LOVE.

GAHHH!

KRASSHH

HE'S NOT ANSWERING!

CRUMPFF

YOU'VE GOT ME ACTING CRAZY, BABY.

RING
RING
YOU GOT ME ACTING WRONG.

WHAT ARE WE WAITING FOR?
WHERE ARE WE SUPPOSED TO GO?
JUST SIT TIGHT. WE HAVE TO WAIT FOR THE BOSS TO CALL.
THUDDD
AAARGH!
WE DON'T MAKE A MOVE WITHOUT THE BOSS.
WHY ISN'T KINGPIG SENDING ANYBODY?
STAG HAWG CAN'T GET AHOLD OF THE KINGPIG! BUT HE HAS TO CALL IN OUR BRUISERS NOW, BECAUSE...
"...PRETTY SOON IT'S GOING TO BE...
"...TOO LATE."
BUHH-WOOOMM!

THAT'S THAT, THEN.
BY THE TIME KINGPIG REBUILDS ALL HIS NIGHTCLUBS, THERE'S GOING TO BE COMPETITION. OTHER CLUBS. OTHER OWNERS.
"HIS STRANGLEHOLD ON NEW YOLK CITY'S ENTERTAINERS IS AT AN END."
I'M TOO NERVOUS. HE'LL KILL US! HE'S GOING TO BE SO ANGRY.
YOU HAVE TO KNOCK.
WE HAVE TO TELL HIM.
KNOCK KNOCK
BOSS?

WE... AHH, WE LOST THE KIT KAT CLUB.
SEE, ME AND THE BOYS WERE WAITING FOR YOUR CALL, AND--
WE DIDN'T KNOW WHAT TO DO! WE'RE SORRY!
DON'T KILL US!
THESE THINGS HAPPEN. THE SITUATION WAS BEYOND YOUR CONTROL. YOU WILL NOT BE PUNISHED.
YOU MAY LEAVE.
WHA...?
IS HE SERIOUS?
I'M NOT SURE! LET'S JUST...
...GET OUT OF HERE!

THE NEXT DAY...
LET ME TELL YOU A STORY
OF A MAN GONE WRONG.
WOW, LISTEN TO THAT! AND LOOK AT ALL THESE PEOPLE!
THIS IS ALL STELLA REALLY WANTED, TO BE ABLE TO SING TO AN AUDIENCE.
BUT ONCE THE NEW NIGHTCLUBS OPEN, IT WON'T BE ANY TROUBLE FOR SOMEONE WITH HER TALENT TO FIND A STARRING ROLE. HER VOICE IS SO BEAUTIFUL.
ALL I KNOW IS I'M CRAZY,
CRAZY, CRAZY FOR YOU.
MAYBE, BABY, MAYBE
YOU'RE CRAZY TOO.
SO... SO BEAUTIFUL...
THE END

ARTWORK BY DAN PARENT